Beowulf

Adapted by
Rob Lloyd Jones

Illustrated by Victor Tavares

Reading consultant: Alison Kelly
Roehampton University

Characters in the story

Beowulf (say Bay-o-wolf)

Grendel

King Hrothgar

Leofric (Lee-of-fritch)

Wiglaf

The Danes

Grendel's mother

The Geats (Jee-ats)

The dragon

Contents

Chapter 1

The great hall

Long, long ago, Denmark was a wild place. Gruesome monsters roamed the misty moors. At night, they howled and growled and shrieked and snarled.

The king of the Danes, a warlord named Hrothgar, refused to be scared. He built a huge hall for himself on top of a craggy hill at the edge of the moors.

The hall was made of the finest wood, decorated with ivory, silver and dazzling gold. The king called it Heorot.

Each night, the king invited his bravest warriors to a lavish feast of roasted meat, with jugs of frothing ale. The huge hall shook with singing and laughter.

The men ate and drank until they fell
asleep, safe together in the warmth.
   But outside, something evil was rising...

Chapter 2

A monster strikes

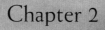

Across the moor, a foul monster crawled from a swamp. Its name was Grendel. It had claws like knives, and burning eyes. The warriors' laughter had woken it from sleep. Grendel hated laughter.

The monster marched across the moors in a fit of rage. It burst upon Heorot and smashed open the doors. The warriors in Heorot were terrified. They had never seen anything so fierce.

The men tried to fight, but Grendel was too strong. The monster snatched up several men and dragged them screaming to its lair at the bottom of the swamp. Heorot dripped with their blood.

Grendel returned every night for months. Any man brave enough to stay in Heorot at night didn't live until morning.

King Hrothgar was heartbroken. At night, his great hall stood silent and empty on the edge of the moors.

Chapter 3

A hero arrives

Across Denmark, a coastguard watched as a warship approached the cliffs. The guard frowned. The ship was filled with Geats, enemies of the Danes.

The guard rushed to challenge the warriors. "Who are you?" he demanded. "What do you want?"

The Geats' leader stepped forward. His shield gleamed in the dazzling sun. "I am Beowulf," he declared. "I have heard the story of Grendel. Tell your king that I have come to kill his monster."

"Go home," the guard insisted, raising his spear. "Many men have died trying to fight Grendel."

Beowulf just smiled. He brushed the guard's spear aside with his palm. "Then that is how I shall die too," he said.

Chapter 4

Final feast

The guard led Beowulf
and the Geats past lakes
and bogs, to where Heorot
towered above the moors.

The Geats were stunned
by the hall's beauty. Beowulf
handed the guard his sword.
"Take my weapon, so your
king knows I come as a friend."

"You'll need it again by nightfall,"
the guard warned. "That's when
Grendel comes."

King Hrothgar sat inside. His face was lined with grief, but he managed a smile to greet the Geats. "You have come far," he said, "to a wild place."

"We have come to kill your monster," Beowulf replied.

The king had heard many men vow to defeat Grendel, and all of them had died. This warrior, though, seemed certain.

"First," said the king, "you must join me for a feast."

The king sent for his warriors from
nearby villages. The Danes and Geats
ate together, swapping stories and
singing songs.

King Hrothgar sighed. The laughter
reminded him of happier times in Heorot.
Beowulf took the king's arm.
"Tomorrow," he promised, "you will hear
laughter again."

Chapter 5

Beowulf v Grendel

Night fell. The hall twinkled with candlelight as King Hrothgar and his men left the Geats to a nervous rest.

Most of the Geats huddled together at the back of the hall, armed with axes, knives and swords. But Beowulf sat alone in a dark corner near the doors.

Beowulf's friend Leofric crawled over. He looked worried. "Beowulf," he whispered, "where is your sword?"

"I gave it to the guard outside," Beowulf replied. "Grendel fights with bare hands, so I will too."

Beowulf saw the fear in his friend's face. "Don't worry Leofric," he added, "we will kill this monster."

An hour passed. Outside on the moors, one of the swamps bubbled. Grendel rose. The beast stomped towards Heorot, dripping with slime and hungry for blood.

Grendel tore open the doors and glared inside. All of the Geats lay fast asleep...

...except for one. Beowulf crouched in the shadows, his steely eyes fixed on the murdering monster.

Grendel reached for Leofric, and
Beowulf pounced, grasping the monster's
arm. Grendel writhed and thrashed, but
Beowulf would not let go.

Grendel swiped and slashed, but
Beowulf would not let go.

The hall shuddered. Benches shattered.
But still Beowulf refused to let go. He
tugged the monster's arm… and tore it
from its body!

Grendel roared in pain. The monster smashed out of the hall and charged into the night, staggering across the moor.

Beowulf stood holding Grendel's dripping arm. He knew the monster would bleed to death. Grendel was defeated.

The next day, Heorot shook with laughter. King Hrothgar hosted a huge feast, and rewarded the Geats with golden treasures. But even as they celebrated Beowulf's victory, something else was stirring out on the moors…

Chapter 6

A new terror

"Beowulf! Come quickly!"
Beowulf woke from a deep sleep, startled by King Hrothgar's cry. He was so tired from his fight with Grendel that he had left Heorot to sleep in a nearby barn. But now he was wide awake.

"What is it?" he asked.

The king's face was pale. His hand shook as he pointed to Heorot. "Another monster," he gasped. "It has killed Leofric."

Beowulf raced to Heorot. The hall was dripping with blood and slime. "But Grendel is dead," Beowulf muttered.

"It wasn't Grendel," one of the Danes told him. "It was his mother."

"We are doomed," said King Hrothgar. "Grendel's mother is pure evil. She lurks at the bottom of the Lake of Demons, in the darkest part of my kingdom."

Beowulf's lips set into a grim line. He slid on his helmet as Wiglaf handed him his sword. "Then that is where I will kill her," he said.

Chapter 7

The Lake of Demons

The Geats sharpened their swords. The Danes gathered their spears. They marched together behind Beowulf, following the monster's tracks to the Lake of Demons.

The Geats had never seen such
a ghastly place. The surface swirled
with ghostly fog. The water was
thick with slime. It was a vile lake.

Beowulf grasped his sword and glared into the dreadful depths.

King Hrothgar followed his gaze into the murky water. "It's so dark down there Beowulf," he whispered. "You do not have to go."

Beowulf just smiled. "That darkness you
see is the monster," he said. "I am the
light." And he dived into the lake.

Beowulf swam down, deeper and
deeper. The water grew thick with slime,
blocking the light from above. Beowulf
kept swimming.

Just as the last ray of light disappeared, something grabbed him. A long tentacle wrapped around Beowulf's waist, dragging him even deeper.

Beowulf rose in a vast underwater
cave, gasping for breath. Stalactites
hung from the ceiling. Skulls
of giants lay scattered
on the rocks.

A gurgling groan echoed around the
cave. Grendel's mother rose from
the foul water.

The monster's eyes shone with hatred. Her slimy tentacles were tipped with sharp talons. "You are the warrior that slew my son," she drooled.

Beowulf tore himself free from the monster's grip. "Yes, I killed Grendel," he declared, "and now I shall kill you."

Beowulf went to attack, but his legs felt suddenly heavy. His sword clattered to the rocks and his head began to spin. The monster had him gripped in a dark spell.

Grendel's mother slithered closer. Beams of blackness shot from her eyes. "I am pure evil," she hissed. "My eyes are pure fear. No man can break free from their spell."

Summoning the last of his strength, Beowulf hurled himself across the rocks and snatched up his sword. "I am not like all men," he roared. "I am Beowulf! And I do not fear you!"

The monster swung her claws.
Beowulf whirled his sword…

Far above, the Geats and Danes waited in worried silence. Beowulf had been gone for too long. King Hrothgar feared that he was dead.

Just then, the water bubbled and frothed. The warriors staggered back in fright as the head of Grendel's mother rose from the lake...

A second later, Beowulf appeared,
gripping the head in his hand.

He held up the trophy, smiling at the
king. "You do not need to be scared
anymore," he cried. "The monster is dead."

47

Beowulf marched with the warriors back to Heorot. The men cheered and joked as dawn blazed across the sky. The great hall looked more beautiful than ever. Its golden roof sparkled in the sun.

Chapter 8

King Beowulf

Beowulf returned to the land of the Geats, where he ruled for fifty years. He led warriors in battles against fierce beasts and savage monsters. All of his enemies feared him – Beowulf, the killer of Grendel.

Beowulf grew old and tired of fighting.
He dreamed of peace. But there was
one last monster left to fight...

Across Beowulf's kingdom, villagers lived in fear of a terrible dragon. At night, the beast swooped over their roofs. Fire roared from its mouth. Houses burned. People ran screaming in the streets.

Beowulf rode to a village near the dragon's lair, where he gathered his warriors in a huge stone hall.

"What can we do?" asked one.

"Fight back!" replied another.

Beowulf sat in silence, gazing around the hall. It reminded him of Heorot, all those years ago. Finally he rose, and the Geats fell silent.

"I will fight this dragon alone," Beowulf declared.

The Geats looked confused. Only Beowulf's cousin Wiglaf dared speak. "Beowulf," he urged, "it is fifty years since you fought Grendel. You're an old man now."

"I am old," Beowulf replied, "and I am tired too. But I have one more fight left in me."

None of the Geats argued. But they were certain their leader would die.

Chapter 9

The last monster

The sun was setting as the warriors approached the dragon's mountain. A huge roar rumbled down the dark slope. The beast had woken.

Wiglaf helped Beowulf into his chainmail. It was the same suit the king had worn to fight Grendel, but now it hung loose around Beowulf's chest.

"Cousin," Wiglaf pleaded to Beowulf, "let me go with you."

Beowulf just stared up the hillside. "I must go alone," he said.

Beowulf clambered up the jagged rock face. The dragon emerged. Its eyes burned like coals. Its tail thrashed against the rocks. Beowulf knew this was the fiercest monster he'd ever faced.

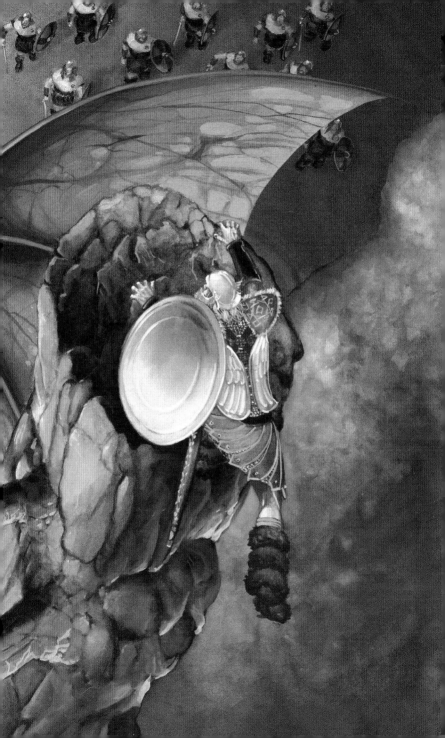

The dragon attacked, spitting fire. Flames swirled around Beowulf's shield.

"I wasn't scared when I fought Grendel," Beowulf cried. "I wasn't scared when I killed his mother. And I am not scared of you."

He lunged at the beast. The dragon twisted and turned in the air. Beowulf dived across the rocks, slashing the monster with his sword.

Just then, Beowulf heard a shout. It was Wiglaf, racing to help him. For a moment, Beowulf's back was turned...

The dragon struck. Its vicious teeth sank into Beowulf's neck.

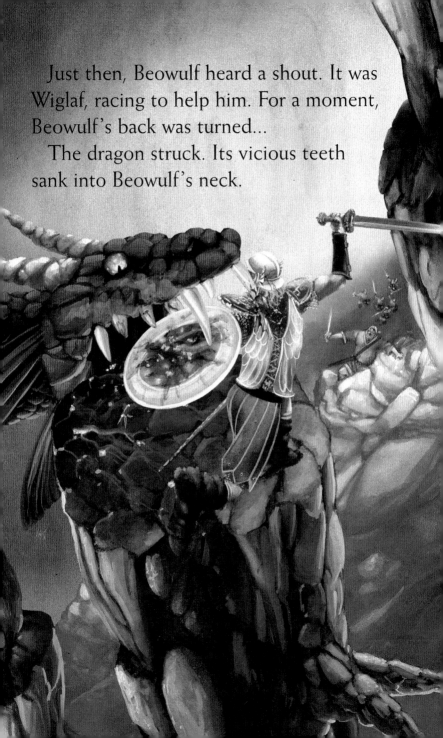

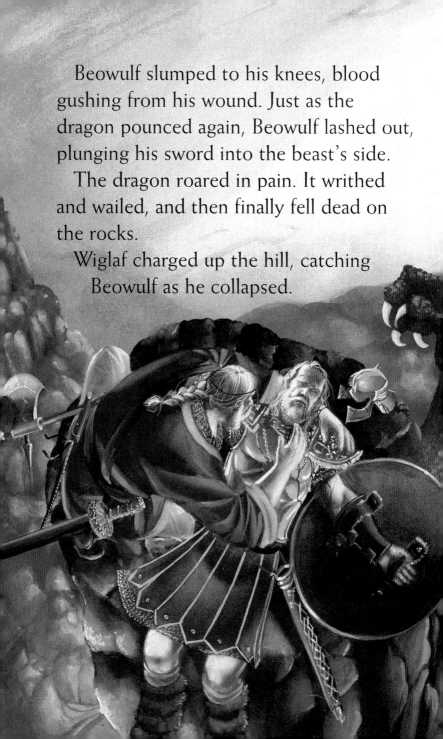

Beowulf slumped to his knees, blood gushing from his wound. Just as the dragon pounced again, Beowulf lashed out, plunging his sword into the beast's side.

The dragon roared in pain. It writhed and wailed, and then finally fell dead on the rocks.

Wiglaf charged up the hill, catching Beowulf as he collapsed.

"Master," Wiglaf cried, pulling off Beowulf's helmet, "it's dead! You have killed the last monster."

For a second, Wiglaf thought he saw Beowulf smile. Then the King of the Geats closed his eyes and died.

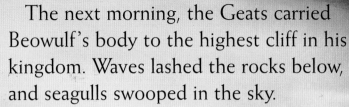

The next morning, the Geats carried Beowulf's body to the highest cliff in his kingdom. Waves lashed the rocks below, and seagulls swooped in the sky.

The warriors placed the king's body to be burned on top of a huge pile of wood. Some of the men cried, others told stories about Beowulf. They knew his name would live forever.

Wiglaf lit the fire and they all said
goodbye to their king. The smoke filled
the sky for miles, but the sun shone
through, bathing the warriors in light.

Internet links

The story of Beowulf was first written
over a thousand years ago in an early form
of English, called Old English. You can find
out more about the story and its origins by
going to the Usborne Quicklinks Website
at www.usborne-quicklinks.com and typing
in the keywords "YR Beowulf".

Please note that Usborne Publishing cannot be responsible
for the content of any website other than its own.

Designed by Michelle Lawrence
Series designer: Russell Punter
Series editor: Lesley Sims

First published in 2009 by Usborne Publishing Ltd., Usborne House,
83-85 Saffron Hill, London EC1N 8RT, England. www.usborne.com
Copyright © 2009 Usborne Publishing Ltd.